When John & Caroline lived in the White House

Happy reading!
Laurie Coulter

by Laurie Coulter

❖

A HYPERION / MADISON PRESS BOOK

First published in the United States by
Hyperion Books for Children
114 Fifth Avenue
New York, New York 10011-5690

9 8 7 6 5 4 3 2 1

Library of Congress Cataloging-in-Publication Data is on file.
ISBN: 0-7868-0624-9

Design and Art Direction: Gordon Sibley Design Inc.
Editorial Director: Hugh Brewster
Editorial Assistance: Susan Aihoshi, Imoinda Romain
Production Director: Susan Barrable
Production Co-ordinator: Sandra L. Hall
Color Separation: Colour Technologies
Printing and Binding: Artegrafica S.p.A.

When John & Caroline lived in the White House was produced by Madison Press Books, which is under the direction of Albert E. Cummings.

Produced by
Madison Press Books
40 Madison Avenue
Toronto, Ontario
Canada M5R 2S1

Printed and bound in Italy

This is the story of Caroline and John Kennedy, Jr., the children of President John F. Kennedy and his wife, Jacqueline. They lived in the White House from February 1961 until November 1963 — a brief but unforgettable time in American history.

A Snowman on the Lawn

"There's lots of room to play and a great big garden, too."

Caroline, after moving into the White House

Caroline skipped down the airplane's steps and ran into her mother's arms. Nanny Maud Shaw followed slowly, carrying tiny two-month-old John, Jr. As snowflakes swirled around them, John and Jacqueline Kennedy quickly led their family across the tarmac and into a waiting limousine.

4

Sandwiched between her parents in the back seat, Caroline chatted happily about all the things she had done at her grandparents' house in Palm Beach, Florida. The three-year-old had weeks of news to tell her father. The last time she had seen him was on television. On January 20, 1961, she had watched as her father was sworn in as president of the United States. Now, Caroline's family was together again. But, best of all, today they were moving into their new home.

As the limousine turned off Pennsylvania Avenue into the White House grounds, a staff policeman opened the Southwest Gate with a smile. At the end of the drive, Caroline could see the presidential mansion. It shone like a snow palace. And right outside, a snowman stood guard with open arms — as if welcoming Caroline and John to the most famous house in the world.

The Kennedy family in the limousine on the way to their new home.

5

1600 Pennsylvania Avenue

"It was difficult on [the children] at first, especially during the first three months when we barely saw them. It almost broke my heart."

Mrs. Kennedy

J. Bernard West, the Chief Usher of the White House, shook hands with Caroline at the Southwest Entrance. As always, he was very calm and dignified, even though his staff had been in an uproar for weeks. They had been helping Mrs. Kennedy redecorate the family quarters on the second floor in time for the children's arrival. A young family hadn't lived there for fifty years — and it showed.

As Mr. West and the Kennedys stepped off the elevator, though, no signs of the dismal dark walls and ugly furniture remained. A pale pink-and-white room waited for Caroline, a bright blue-and-white nursery for John, and a bedroom between the two for Miss Shaw. A small dining room, kitchen, and pantry had been added as well. Caroline's mother had thought of everything, even a wicker wastebasket for Miss Shaw's banana peels!

Even so, like any new house, the White House seemed strange at first. Mrs. Kennedy complained that it was like living in a hotel. A butler, a maid, and a cook had worked for the Kennedys in their Georgetown house, but hundreds of people bustled about the White House. Unfamiliar faces kept popping in and out of the family's rooms — carrying sheets and towels, balancing silver trays of food, bringing messages and folders to Caroline's parents. It was a very busy place.

(Opposite) The new First Family pauses at the Southwest Entrance.
(Above) Caroline liked taking care of her baby brother, who sometimes napped in his carriage on the Truman balcony.

7

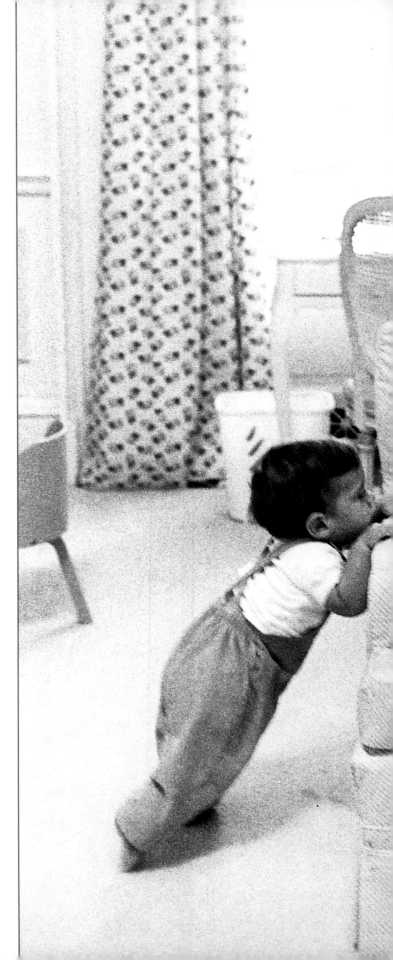

(Above) President Kennedy
and Caroline visit Miss Shaw
and John in his new bedroom.
(Left) Caroline owned a large
Raggedy Ann doll, like this
one, called "Mother Annie."
In a later photograph of the
children taken in Caroline's
room (right), the doll's head
pokes up behind the red-and-
white loveseat. Robin, the
canary, looks on from
his cage.

Caroline enjoyed playing with her baby brother (above and opposite) in her new bedroom. (Right) As a photographer takes her picture, she takes one of him.

By bedtime, Mr. West and most of the staff had left for the night. In the black quiet of Caroline's room, the walls soared up into the darkness and disappeared. Although her canopy bed made a cozy space within the enormous bedroom, Caroline asked Miss Shaw to leave her door open. When the nanny asked why, she said, "Oh, Miss Shaw, I always feel that if you close the door, maybe you won't be able to open it again quickly if I want you."

Miss Shaw understood. "All right, darling. We'll leave it open. You know I'll come if you call."

Working in the White House

- 70 men and women — from doormen and maids to cooks and carpenters — worked for J. B. West, the Chief Usher. He and his staff looked after the central part of the 132-room mansion — from the state rooms on the first floor to the six guest bedrooms on the third floor.
  - 300 people — from aides and press officers to secretaries and telephone operators — worked with President Kennedy in the West Wing and Mrs. Kennedy in the East Wing.
    - 200 special police officers and a squad of Secret Service agents protected the White House and the First Family.

(Far left) Chef René Verdon; (above) Secret Service agent, Bob Foster, with Caroline; (center) Chief Usher J. B. West; (below) Mrs. Kennedy's press secretary, Pam Turnure, with Caroline's cat, Tom Kitten.

Kennedy Mania

"I don't want them to think they are 'official' children. When I go out with them or when they go out with their nurse, please ask the doorman not to hover around to open the doors for them."

Mrs. Kennedy gives instructions to Mr. West

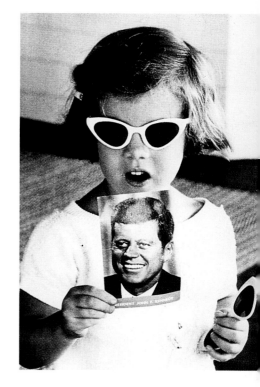

Once they moved into the White House, Caroline and John became as famous as the house they lived in. More than a million people a year began touring the White House in 1961, hoping to catch a glimpse of them, their handsome father, or their glamorous mother. Three hundred fan letters a day poured into the East Wing. What kind of baby food did Jacqueline Kennedy feed to her son? they asked. And what color lipstick did she wear? One fan even sent a portrait of "Jackie" made of sticky caramel corn with a red nail polish smile!

Every week, dolls and toy horses for Caroline and stuffed animals for John filled the mailroom. Real animals began arriving as well, including Zsa Zsa the rabbit. (She apparently could play a few notes of the "Star Spangled Banner" on a toy horn and liked to drink beer!) Mrs. Kennedy's staff patiently answered each letter and gave the toys to a children's hospital and the animals to the zoo.

Caroline, holding a picture of her father, poses like a movie star. JFK and Jackie sun masks (opposite) and the "Caroline doll" (right) joined a long list of toys, records, and games about the First Family.

All this attention could have been overwhelming. But Mrs. Kennedy wanted a "simple, unspoiled, normal life" for Caroline and John, away from the intruding cameras of photographers and tourists. She set up a school in the third-floor sunroom of the White House for Caroline's playgroup from the family's old neighborhood. Then she designed a private playground for the children under the trees near the President's office. "Let's put in a trampoline right there," she suggested to Mr. West. "And hide it somehow, please." After the gardeners planted tall holly trees around the trampoline, she said, "Oh this will be perfect! Now, when I jump on the trampoline, all they'll be able to see is my head, sailing up above the tree tops!"

Good Morning, Miss Shaw!

"Only after we had taken the smoothly operated elevator to the second floor did I feel that we were 'away from it all' in our own little kingdom."

Miss Shaw

"Step on a crack, break your mother's back" — President Kennedy helps Caroline jump over the cracks along the West Wing's colonnade (above) and plays with John outside the Oval Office (opposite).

By the end of Caroline and John's first year in the White House, their family had settled into a daily routine.

7:00 – 9:30 AM

Early every morning, the children visited Miss Shaw in her room, ate breakfast in the upstairs kitchen, then scooted down the hallway to their father's room. By that time, President Kennedy had eaten his own breakfast and read six newspapers and several government reports. He could read 2,400 words a minute! They watched cartoons on television or played with little toy ducks and pigs in their father's bathwater. After leaving John with Mrs. Kennedy, Caroline and the President walked to his office in the West Wing.

9:30 AM – 12:30 PM

At 9:30, Caroline joined her friends in the schoolroom for the morning. Mrs. Kennedy took John outside for an hour, then worked at her desk until lunch. She wrote letters, planned dinners for important visitors, and worked on her special project — redecorating the White House. Miss Shaw took John to play in his room or in the wide center hall upstairs.

In 1962, more than 46 million Americans watched Mrs. Kennedy's one-hour television tour of the White House. In it, the First Lady showed viewers the beautiful antiques she and her committee had collected for the state rooms.

"John is a bad, squeaky boy who tries to spit in his mother's Coca-Cola and who has a very bad temper."

Caroline writes a letter to her grandmother, Rose Kennedy

The South Lawn was the perfect place to play on the swings (above) or have a picnic (opposite). Mrs. Kennedy enjoyed finding places for her children to play and even wondered if the White House bomb shelter could be used for a basketball court!

12:30 — 1:30 PM

Until Caroline began to go to school for the entire day, the children ate lunch upstairs with Mrs. Kennedy or had a picnic on the South Lawn.

1:30 — 3:00 PM

After a dip in the indoor pool, President Kennedy arrived home for his lunch and a nap. The staff left the family apartment, the phones stopped ringing, and the children and their parents slept.

3:00 — 6:00 PM

In the afternoon, Caroline and John played upstairs or out on the playground. Sometimes they watched a movie with friends in their own private theater in the basement of the East Wing. And on hot days, they waded in the South Fountain — the best wading pool in the city — squealing as the cool gushes of water splashed over their heads.

Caroline, shown here playing in the family quarters upstairs, liked *Bambi* so much that her mother asked Mr. West if they could keep deer on the grounds. But the National Zoo told him that the deer would be able to jump right over the White House fence.

6:00 — 6:30 PM

The children ate dinner with Miss Shaw. During her second week in the White House, Caroline had turned up her nose at the meals made by the chefs. Liver three times in four days! Fortunately, Miss Shaw planned the meals after that. If something new was served, she simply said, "Now, you just try one spoonful. If you really don't like it, leave the rest. But the next time you have it, try two spoonfuls." Even spinach soon disappeared from the children's plates using the English nanny's technique.

6:30 — 8:00 PM

Mrs. Kennedy read to Caroline and John after their dinner. Sometimes she let them take a bubble bath in her bathroom as a special treat. While their mother put on dressy clothes for dinner with the President and their guests, Caroline and John tumbled about her room.

On other days, the children joined their father for his evening swim. Or, if no

official guests were dining with them, the Kennedys and their friends liked to watch the latest Hollywood movies. Caroline and John were allowed to watch until bedtime.

8:00 PM

Miss Shaw read stories to the children and helped them say their prayers. Then their parents came in to give them a good-night kiss and to tuck them into bed.

During their games of tag in the pool, John liked to call his father silly names like "Foo-Foo Head." Reporters once heard the President calling his son, "John... John...," and assumed his son's nickname was "John-John," but it wasn't.

"Thank you, for the world so sweet.
Thank you, for the food we eat.
Thank you, for the birds that sing.
Thank you, God, for everything."

Miss Shaw taught this prayer to Caroline and John

(Above) In his room before bedtime, John plays with his mother's pearl necklace and shakes hands with a large toy nutcracker. Caroline (left) is still wearing one of the costumes from her dress-up box. On another evening (opposite), Miss Shaw waits for the President and John to return from the Oval Office.

School on the Third Floor

"Somebody's been up here making the biggest mess! And it's not the first time, either. Something is going on in this nursery school at night!"

Miss Grimes complains to Mr. West

The young teacher, Miss Grimes, stared at the sand scattered around the shiny linoleum floor. Caroline's cat, Tom Kitten, had never liked the White House and now lived with the President's secretary, so he hadn't made the mess. The rabbits were nibbling lettuce in their cages. Caroline's escape-artist hamsters, Billie and Debbie, rarely scampered beyond the President's bathroom. And Charlie, the Welsh terrier, slept in a room on the ground floor. So who was it?

After talking to Miss Grimes, the Chief Usher asked one of the maids to come to his office. Did she know who or what was digging in the sandbox? "It's just Mrs. Kennedy and Caroline," she replied with a smile. "They come up here at night and play in the sand." In the end, nobody could blame them. The schoolroom's big sandbox — as well as its spectacular view and shelves of books, toys, and art supplies — made it the best playroom in the house.

Mrs. Kennedy joins her daughter and a friend (above) crayoning at a table.
(Left) Caroline's crayons.
(Opposite) Caroline stands fifth from the right in the second row of her school photo.

How do you tell if
there's an elephant
in your refrigerator?
By the footprints
in the pudding.

(Above) Children told lots of elephant jokes
in the 1960s. (On this page) Caroline sews,
answers a question, and reads in the
schoolroom. (Opposite) A Halloween party
and a performance in an upstairs hallway.

The Space Race

On April 12, 1961, Russian cosmonaut Yuri Gagarin became the first person to orbit the earth. Although President Kennedy congratulated the Soviet Union on its "outstanding technical accomplishment," he and other Americans feared that the Soviets would soon dominate the earth from space. They hurried to catch up, sending Alan Shepard into space on May 5, 1961. After this success, President Kennedy vowed to put a man on the moon before the decade was over. The American space program moved into high gear, and on February 20, 1962, John Glenn became the first American to orbit Earth.

The children always welcomed visitors to their school, whether a group of Native Americans in traditional costume or parents for a picnic (opposite).

Astronaut John Glenn shows President Kennedy the *Mercury-Atlas 6* spacecraft in which he orbited the earth three times.

In the spring of 1962, the ten children in Caroline's playgroup were ready for nursery school or kindergarten, depending upon their ages. The school expanded to twenty-one children. To help Miss Grimes, the parents hired another teacher, Jacqueline Hirsh.

Mrs. Kennedy asked the teachers not to treat her daughter any differently than the other children. On field trips to museums or to the National Gallery of Art, Caroline's Secret Service agents tagged along, but the two men didn't hold Caroline's hand and they kept their walkie-talkies out of sight. When her class watched special ceremonies on the South Lawn, Caroline lined up with everyone else. And when they were invited to meet an astronaut, the President's daughter joined the other excited children reaching out to shake their hero's hand.

Pushinka and Charlie

> **"It is a pleasure to fulfill Mrs. Kennedy's wish and to send to you and your family little Pushinka...."**
>
> Soviet leader Nikita Khrushchev sends a gift to the Kennedys

At the family's summer home in Hyannisport, John and his mother hold Shannon and two puppies, while Clipper stands, Wolf sprawls on the patio, and Charlie plays with Caroline.

Pushinka, which means "fluffy" in Russian, joined Charlie at the White House in June, 1961. A year earlier, her famous mother, Strelka, had orbited the earth in the Russian satellite *Sputnik*. Clearly a space-dog's daughter, Pushinka loved launching herself from the playground's slide. Charlie, meanwhile, chased the ducks in the fountain or

28

nipped the gardeners as they bent over the flower beds.

Charlie and Pushinka had four puppies — Blackie, White Tips, Butterfly, and Streaker. The Kennedy dog family had now grown to nine! After Pushinka, three more canine gifts arrived: Wolf, an Irish wolfhound; Clipper, a German shepherd; and Shannon, a cocker spaniel.

Even for a family of animal lovers, this was too many dogs. Mrs. Kennedy and the Press Office organized a letter-writing contest. Children were asked to write why they could provide a good home for a Kennedy puppy. Ten thousand children entered the contest and the two winners each received a puppy. The remaining two puppies were adopted by relatives.

The Cold War

During the Kennedy years, there was great tension between the United States, with its democratic form of government, and the Soviet Union, with its communist system. Soviet and American troops didn't fight on a battleground, but both countries spent huge amounts of money building nuclear weapons to use against each other if war began. President Kennedy and Premier Khrushchev met on June 3, 1961, in Vienna to try and build some trust between their two nations. It was after this meeting that Premier Khrushchev sent Pushinka to the Kennedys.

Although Charlie (above left) was the Kennedys' first dog, Shannon (left) became the family favorite. Soviet leader Nikita Khrushchev gave Pushinka (above right) to Mrs. Kennedy after he met her in Vienna (far right).

29

Special Days

"The chopper's coming, Miss Shaw! The chopper's coming!"

John

Meeting Oval Office visitors (above right) was fun, but watching them land in the presidential helicopter was even better. John loved helicopters. Sometimes he and his father would sit at the controls and pretend to fly the chopper together. (Opposite) Mrs. Kennedy and John watch the welcoming ceremony for the President of Algeria.

On October 15, 1962, Caroline and her schoolfriends watched the arrival of the first foreign leader ever brought to the White House by helicopter. "Here it comes!" they shouted, as the chopper clattered straight towards them. A few minutes later, it had landed like a giant insect on the lawn.

President Kennedy stepped forward to welcome His Excellency Ahmed Ben Bella, the President of Algeria. The two men stood at attention during the solemn military welcoming ceremony, which included a thunderous twenty-one-gun salute. On the balcony, the excited children marched about loudly, copying the many soldiers parading below. Unfortunately, they didn't stop when the President gave his speech.

The next day, an article appeared in the *Washington Post* newspaper about the children's antics. Poor Miss Grimes and Miss Hirsh, who didn't think their students could be heard, quickly wrote letters of apology to the President.

This was one of the few times that his daughter or son embarrassed President Kennedy. The children "knew exactly how to behave on formal occasions," boasted Miss Shaw. "As soon as they were old enough, Caroline was taught to curtsy and John to bow...."

An Empress
Comes to Call

Before state dinners, the President and Mrs. Kennedy entertained visiting heads of state in the Yellow Oval Room. Like other parents, they liked to introduce their children to their dinner guests. In the past year, John and Caroline had met princes, princesses, governors, and other dignitaries.

"It was terribly exciting for a little girl to see all the people dressed in their evening dresses, glittering with jewelry...." said Miss Shaw.

The most glittering guest of all arrived on April 11, 1962, with the visit of the Shah of Iran and his wife, Farah Diba, who wore a diamond tiara and a necklace studded with emeralds.

On the afternoon of the 1962 state dinner for the Iranian royal couple (opposite), Mrs. Kennedy introduces the Empress of Iran to John, while Caroline's pony, Macaroni, looks on (below right). After state dinners, guests watched a show in the East Room. President Kennedy talks to opera singer Grace Bumbry (above right) after her performance.

Foreign Trips

President Kennedy met foreign leaders in their own countries as well as at the White House. Wherever he and Mrs. Kennedy traveled, people thronged to see the handsome, young American president and his elegant wife. People everywhere were tired of war, and President Kennedy's passionate speeches about peace filled them with hope for the future.

While their mother was away in France (above) or in India with her sister, Lee Radziwill (right), Caroline and John received a postcard from her every day. In August 1962, Caroline traveled abroad for the first time — to Italy with her mother (left).

(Above) Jacqueline Kennedy meets a Royal Canadian Mounted Police officer during a state visit to Ottawa. (Below) In 1963, President Kennedy looks out over the Berlin Wall. In a famous speech, the President said, "Ich bin ein Berliner" ("I'm a Berliner"), meaning that he would always support democracy in the divided city of Berlin.

John & Caroline's

Ground Floor

1. Library
2. Ground Floor Corridor
3. Vermeil Room
4. China Room
5. Diplomatic Reception Room
6. Map Room
7. Southwest Entrance
8. To the West Wing
9. To the East Wing

State Floor

10. East Room
11. Green Room
12. Blue Room
13. Red Room
14. State Dining Room
15. Family Dining Room
16. Cross Hall
17. Entrance Hall

(Top) The schoolroom on the third floor. (Above) Mrs. Kennedy stands on the Truman balcony with the Washington Monument in the background. (Below) Visitors try out the seats in the movie theater in the basement of the East Wing.

White House

(Above) The President (in the rocking chair) and Mrs. Kennedy entertain a group of astronauts and their wives in the Yellow Oval Room.

(Right) Caroline and her mother sit in on a rehearsal for the musical *Brigadoon*, which would be performed for the King of Morocco that evening. Special performances were given in the East Room after dinners held for world leaders.

Daddy's Office

**"My Daddy is President; what does your Daddy do?
I live in a big white house on Pennsylvania Avenue.
I always hide behind the desk in Daddy's den
When I play hide-and-seek with Secret Service men."**

From the song, "My Daddy Is President," recorded in 1962 by Little Jo Ann

Caroline rummaged through Mrs. Lincoln's desk drawer. "Do you have anything for me?" she asked her father's secretary. Evelyn Lincoln always had a particularly long rubber band or something equally special to take back upstairs to show Mommy.

That evening, Caroline and John were waiting in the secretary's office for their father to finish his work. While Mrs. Lincoln set up meetings on the phone and wrote letters, John twirled around on a swivel chair and Caroline practiced typing her name on the typewriter. Each time she banged on a key, a letter appeared on the paper in the machine. Her long name took a long time.

If she had been tall enough, Caroline could have looked through the peephole in the door between the two offices to see what her father was doing. Finally, though, the door opened. The President came out, acting very surprised.

"Hello there, Sam, how are you?" he teased John.

"I am not Sam, I'm John. Daddy, I'm John."

Next he turned to Caroline, "Hello there, Mary."

John ran past him, opened the secret panel in his father's old desk and squeezed into the space behind it. One day the little boy hid there while President Kennedy began an important meeting with a British politician. Suddenly John jumped out, shouting, "I'm a big bear and I'm hungry!"

As John giggled, the President laughed and said to his surprised visitor, "You may think this is strange behavior in the office of the President of the United States, but in addition to being the President, I also happen to be a father."

Playing "going under the mountain" on the colonnade (opposite), hiding in the secret "cave" in the President's desk (above), and visiting Mrs. Lincoln (below).

Caroline and John dance in the Oval Office (opposite). Then John takes a ride in his father's rocking chair (above left). (Above right) Caroline as a witch and John as "Peter Panda" try to scare their father on Halloween.

A Dream for the Future

In 1960, many African Americans had voted for John F. Kennedy, the Democratic Party's candidate. They hoped he would change the unfair laws in the South that forced them to attend separate schools, eat in separate areas in restaurants, and sit in the backs of buses. On August 28, 1963, 200,000 people marched in support of civil rights in the March on Washington. On that day, Martin Luther King, Jr., gave his famous "I have a dream" speech, in which he said, "I have a dream that my four little children will one day live in a nation where they will not be judged by the color of their skin but by the content of their character." He and other civil rights leaders then met with President Kennedy in the Oval Office. Later that year, the President proposed civil rights legislation to give all Americans equal opportunity in education, employment, and voting. Most of the President's suggestions were enacted in the Civil Rights Act of 1964.

Martin Luther King, Jr., stands fourth from the left in this group of civil rights leaders who met President Kennedy after the March on Washington.

The Cuban Missile Crisis

President Kennedy's children often took his mind off the important decisions he had to make every day. At the school's mid-morning recess, the President would sometimes clap his hands outside the Oval Office to get Caroline's attention. She and her friends, and John when he was older, would run over from the playground for a visit.

On a Monday morning in October 1962, the President clapped his hands for Caroline even though he was in the middle of a

Caroline and two schoolfriends say hello to the President before going to visit Mrs. Lincoln's candy jar.

"But I have to."

Caroline pushed open the door and blurted out, "Daddy, I would have come sooner, but Miss Grimes wouldn't let me go."

The tension briefly drained from the faces of the men working around the large table. The President smiled, too, and said, "That's all right, Caroline." And with that, she skipped off to play.

At seven o'clock that night, a grim-faced President appeared on television. He told Americans about the missiles and said that he had

terrible crisis. American spy planes had taken pictures of Soviet nuclear missiles under construction in Cuba. For the first time, weapons of mass destruction were within striking range of most of the United States.

When Caroline didn't appear, he strolled back into the Cabinet Room to meet once more with his top government advisors.

Mrs. Lincoln remembers Caroline flying into his empty office a few minutes later.

"He's in a meeting in the Cabinet Room," she told Caroline, "but I wouldn't go in there."

demanded their removal. American battleships would stop the Soviet Union from delivering any more weapons to Cuba.

The world waited in fear. Premier Khrushchev was furious about the naval blockade. Work continued on the missile sites, as messages and telephone calls flew between the Oval Office and the Kremlin in Moscow. Days went by and still the Soviet Union refused to back down and remove the missiles. War seemed inevitable.

Some people stocked food and water in underground bomb shelters in their backyards. Others put sandbags against basement walls, hoping to survive a nuclear attack in their

President Kennedy prepares to address the nation. Rather than send in the armed forces to remove the missiles in Cuba, he told Americans he was ordering a naval blockade. His calm response to the crisis prevented a war.

The Hot Line

After the Cuban Missile Crisis, President Kennedy and Premier Khrushchev set up a special telephone line between their offices. They hoped the Hot Line would stop a war from beginning by mistake. The red phone in the Oval Office had no dial, unlike this toy phone from the period. The President simply picked up the receiver and was immediately connected to the Kremlin.

cellars. Plans were made to fly the President and his advisors, if necessary, to a secret bomb shelter. They would run the government from there if Washington were bombed. Their families, though, could not go with them. President Kennedy urged his wife to think about taking the children out of the city to the shelter for White House employees' families. She chose to stay with him in Washington.

On Friday, October 26, President Kennedy received a long letter from the Soviet leader. It contained the first hope of a peaceful settlement to the crisis. The next day, the United States promised not to attempt to overthrow Cuba's communist government if the Soviet Union removed its missiles. Khrushchev agreed and the thirteen-day Cuban Missile Crisis was over. But the world had come closer to the brink of nuclear war than it ever had before.

My Pony, Macaroni

Macaroni, Caroline's piebald pony with the white "booties," became the most famous Kennedy animal. He received his own fan letters from children, and one man even wrote a hit song about him called, "My Pony, Macaroni."

Macaroni turned up in some strange places. The President was very proud of his new garden just outside the Oval Office. But Macaroni treated the Rose Garden as his personal salad bar. After many stern presidential warnings, the pony was banned from freely wandering about the grounds.

(Top) John, Caroline, and Macaroni meet the President outside the Oval Office. (Middle) Macaroni takes Jacqueline Kennedy and her children for a sleigh ride on the White House lawn. (Bottom) Mrs. Kennedy and John on Sardar and Caroline on Macaroni go for a morning ride at their country home in Virginia. The family spent many weekends at Glen Ora. (Right) Paper dolls of Caroline and her mother in riding clothes. (Opposite page) Macaroni lived in a shed on the White House grounds when Caroline wasn't riding him.

Holidays and Birthdays

"... birthdays, Christmases, Easters. These had always been special family times for the Kennedys, when games and fun were more important than presents."

Hugh Sidey, a family friend

In the children's 1962 nativity play (below left), Caroline was Mary, her cousin Christina Radziwill was an angel, and Gustavo Parades, the son of Mrs. Kennedy's personal maid, played Joseph. Hanging stockings (below right) and playing with John (opposite).

A few weeks after the Cuban Missile Crisis, President Kennedy lit the nation's Christmas tree on the Ellipse, the park across from the White House. Caroline and John spent that happy Christmas of 1962 with their parents in Palm Beach, Florida. The family always spent the Christmas and Easter holidays there. During the summer holidays, they joined their grandparents, eight aunts and uncles, and nineteen cousins at the Kennedy family's seaside "compound" in Hyannisport on Cape Cod.

Palm Beach, Florida

"For John, there was the sea and the sand.... He scampered and splashed, built sandcastles and demolished them with ferocious gusto — though he would get awfully mad if anyone else tampered with them."

Miss Shaw

(Above left) Decorating Easter eggs in the kitchen of Joseph and Rose Kennedy's Palm Beach home. (Above right) A family portrait taken after Easter services in 1963. (Below) Mrs. Kennedy and Clipper play with John on the beach.

White House Birthdays

May 29, 1917

John Fitzgerald Kennedy

July 28, 1929

Jacqueline Bouvier Kennedy

November 27, 1957

Caroline Bouvier Kennedy

November 25, 1960

John Fitzgerald Kennedy, Jr.

(Left) Chef Verdon shows off his birthday cake for the President. (Top and middle) The children's parties were held in the President's Dining Room. (Bottom) A member of the United States Marine Band plays with John. Balloons decorate one of the trikes used in the birthday tricycle races.

Hyannisport, Massachusetts

"One day he was sitting on the stern of the *Honey Fitz* telling [Caroline] another whale story, and Franklin Roosevelt, Jr., was sitting beside him with his legs crossed and his shoes off....

As the President told the story, he said that one of the delicacies the whale liked the most was old, dirty sweatsocks; and he reached over and grabbed one off of Franklin's foot and threw it over the stern. The President kept on with the story, saying that the only thing the whale liked more was a second sock; and he reached over and took the second sock off and threw it over the stern. Caroline watched with absolute rapt fascination as the socks disappeared into the water, because she thought the whale had [eaten] them."

William Walton, a family friend, quoted in *John Fitzgerald Kennedy*

(Above) A 1960s postcard of the Kennedys' summer home. (Right) Caroline and her father on the yacht *Honey Fitz*. (Opposite) John at the wheel of a motorboat.

Their Last Months Together

"I suddenly felt the President standing beside me. He wasn't saying a thing, just looking up in the sky.... I had the strangest feeling. I couldn't explain it — eerie, like a warning."

Mrs. Lincoln, November 13, 1963

At Hyannisport, in the sunny summer of 1963, Caroline and John entered swimming races at the West Beach club, played miniature golf, and cooked hotdogs over bonfires on the beach. Near the house, they played ball and ran noisy races with Bob Foster and the other Secret Service men. But inside, the two children tried to be as quiet as possible. Their mother lay in bed recovering from the premature birth, and the death two days later, of their baby brother, Patrick. It was a very sad time for John and Caroline's parents.

By mid-September, when Mrs. Kennedy returned to Washington with the children, she was feeling better. The family's familiar routine began again. John joined Caroline at the upstairs school. The President traveled across the country giving speeches, and Mrs. Kennedy left for a short cruise in the Mediterranean. At home, more foreign heads of state visited, adding more pint-size national costumes to the children's huge dress-up box.

On November 21, John's parents took him along on the short helicopter ride to Andrews Air Force Base. From there, they were flying to Texas aboard the presidential jet, *Air Force One*. The President sat down in the seat opposite his son's and began gently tapping John's foot with his own. "Don't, Daddy." A little while later, another little kick. "Don't, Daddy!" Then giggles. It was the last time they would play one of their favorite games. As his parents boarded *Air Force One*, John returned to the White House in the helicopter with Miss Shaw.

(Below) The President and his son wave good-bye from the presidential helicopter.

(Opposite) John marches with his father following a Veterans Day ceremony at Arlington National Cemetery on November 11, 1963.

53

After visiting Fort Worth, the Kennedys flew to Dallas on November 22. At the airport, an open-topped limousine waited to carry the Kennedys into the city. As it reached downtown Dallas, the twenty-car presidential motorcade moved slowly through the cheering crowds lining the streets. The President and Mrs. Kennedy waved happily.

Suddenly, three shots rang out. The President slumped into his wife's lap. Bystanders threw themselves onto the ground, covering their children's bodies with their own. The President's car slammed to a stop, as screams filled the air. A Secret Service agent leaped from the car behind. Mrs. Kennedy crawled onto the limousine's back deck, reached out her hand, and pulled him into the car. Then they raced to the hospital.

Afterwards, people around the world remembered where they were when they first heard the shocking news. Evelyn Lincoln was in the motorcade. J. B. West was listening to the radio at home. Maud Shaw had just tucked John and Caroline into their beds for their naps. She was in the upstairs hallway of the White House when Bob Foster, his eyes full of tears, told her, "The President is dead."

(Opposite) Caroline, the President, and John watch a performance of the Black Watch Highland Regiment on November 13, 1963. (Above) The Kennedys meet well-wishers at the Dallas airport on the last day of the President's life. (Below) The presidential motorcade.

The Saddest Birthday

"...John thought when he heard the helicopters that it was his father coming home."

Social Secretary Nancy Tuckerman remembers the night of November 22

What's the matter, Miss Shaw? Why are you crying?"

"I can't help crying, Caroline, because I have some very sad news to tell you."

She gathered the little girl in her arms and told her that her father had died.

When it seemed as though she couldn't possibly cry anymore, Caroline fell asleep. Miss Shaw slipped out of the room, leaving the door open a little — as always.

In the morning, Mrs. Kennedy came sadly into the nursery and hugged her children. John was too young to understand much of what was happening. The next day he went with his mother and sister to the Capitol building where the President's body lay in state. Mrs. Kennedy and Caroline solemnly walked inside the Rotunda and knelt beside the flag-draped coffin to pray and say good-bye. John stayed outside in the hallway with Maud Shaw and Bob Foster.

While they waited, Miss Shaw and Mr. Foster took John for a walk around the building. In one of the offices, a guide asked the little boy if he would like one of the miniature flags pinned on a board. "Yes, please," he said. "And one for my sister, please." Then he hesitated. "Please, may I have one for Daddy?"

(Above left) Caroline and her mother pray beside the President's coffin in the Capitol Rotunda (opposite). (Above right) Mrs. Kennedy and her children leave the White House on their way to the Capitol.

"Your father has gone to look after Patrick. Patrick was so lonely in heaven. He didn't know anybody there. Now he has the best friend anybody could have."

Miss Shaw

Drumbeats and the quiet sobs of the thousands lining the route were the only sounds heard during the President's funeral procession. (Left) Mrs. Kennedy and her children watch as the horse-drawn caisson bearing the coffin (top) and the black riderless horse (above), the symbol of a fallen leader, pass by. In one of the most famous photographs of the past century, John salutes his father's coffin (opposite).

"Did he take the big plane with him? I wonder when he's coming back."

John

On November 25, the flag John chose for his father and a farewell letter from Caroline were buried with the President in Arlington National Cemetery. It was John's third birthday. About a week after the funeral, Mrs. Kennedy held a small birthday party for both children. They each invited eight friends. As noise and laughter filled the room, Mrs. Kennedy turned to Miss Shaw and said quietly, "I'm glad they are happy."

Many foreign heads of state attended President Kennedy's funeral. Jacqueline Kennedy receives their condolences in the Red Room (above). Eleven days later (opposite), she left the White House with her children.

Finally, the day came to say good-bye to the White House. Only Shannon, the President's favorite dog, would be going with them to their new home. (The rest of the dogs had been adopted by Mr. Foster, the head gardener, and relatives.) On December 6, as their car reached the Southwest Gate, Caroline and John looked for Pete, their favorite policeman.

"Where's Pete?" Caroline asked her mother and Miss Shaw.

"I expect he's off duty today," the nanny said, with tears in her eyes.

"Oh, I wish I could wave good-bye to him," Caroline said as the limousine turned onto Pennsylvania Avenue.

Epilogue

John and Caroline with their mother and Caroline's husband, Edwin Schlossberg, at the 1993 opening of the museum at the John F. Kennedy Library in Boston.

After they left the White House, Jacqueline Kennedy and her two children continued to fascinate the public. When newspapers and magazines printed untrue stories about John and Caroline, their mother said, "Just remember who you are and remember how proud your father was and would have been, and never forget that."

They never did. Today, Caroline Kennedy Schlossberg, who is a lawyer, has written two books on legal matters and is the mother of three children. John F. Kennedy, Jr., also graduated from law school. After working as an assistant district attorney in New York City, John became the publisher of a magazine about politics called *George*. They both worked hard to raise funds for the John F. Kennedy Library and Museum and other charitable causes.

At Caroline's wedding to Edwin Schlossberg in 1986, her brother gave a moving toast: "All of our lives, there's been just the three of us — Mommy, Caroline, and I. Now there's a fourth." Sadly, his mother died in 1994 at the age of 65. Five years later John also died. The small plane he was flying crashed into the ocean, instantly killing him, his wife Carolyn, and his sister-in-law Lauren Bessette.

Only Caroline remains of the four Kennedys who lived in the White House during that time known as "the thousand days" — a thousand days of special memories to be shared with her own children, Tatiana, Rose, and John.

Glossary

Berlin Wall: In 1961, a wall was built between East and West Berlin to prevent East Germans from escaping to West Germany. It became a symbol of communist oppression. The wall was torn down in 1990 when Germany became one country again.

bomb shelter: An underground room strong enough to protect the people inside from a bomb exploding nearby.

Capitol: The building in Washington where the House of Representatives and the Senate meet.

communist system of government: A type of government in which the governing party controls all farms, factories, and businesses and, to a large extent, the social and cultural lives of the people as well.

cosmonaut: An astronaut of the Soviet space program.

democratic system of government: A type of government in which the people vote for candidates from competing political parties in regularly held elections. The party that wins the election forms the government.

district attorney: A government official who brings legal action in court against people accused of a crime.

Georgetown: An area in the western part of Washington, D.C.

Kremlin: The buildings in the city of Moscow that serve as the center of the Russian government.

nuclear missile: A weapon carrying a nuclear warhead, which is launched into the air at a distant target.

piebald pony: A pony with patches of different colors.

Secret Service agents: The government employees who protect the president and his family.

Soviet Union: Once the world's largest country, the Union of Soviet Socialist Republics (USSR) existed from 1917 to 1991, when it broke apart. Its fifteen republics, including Russia, were controlled by a central communist government in Moscow.

walkie-talkie: A small receiving and transmitting radio set.

Index

Picture Credits

Every effort has been made to correctly attribute all material reproduced in this book. If any errors have occurred, we will be happy to correct them in future editions.

All photographs, unless otherwise credited, are from the collection of the John F. Kennedy Library and Museum, Boston, Massachusetts.

3: © Corbis
4,5: © Terry Ashe/Liaison Agency; (inset p. 4) AP/Wide World Photos; (inset p. 5) Archive Photos
6: © Corbis
7: (left) © Corbis; (right) © The Mark Shaw Collection/Photo Researchers, Inc.
8, 9: (top and middle) © The Mark Shaw Collection/Photo Researchers, Inc.; (below) Private Collection; (right) © The Mark Shaw Collection/Photo Researchers, Inc.

10: (above left and right) © The Mark Shaw Collection/Photo Researchers, Inc.; (below) © Bettmann/Corbis
11: © The Mark Shaw Collection/Photo Researchers, Inc.
12: Bob Halmi/Life Magazine © Time Inc.
13: (above) © Stanley Tretick/Corbis Sygma; (below) Courtesy of Strong Museum, Rochester, New York © 2000
14: (left) Paul Schutzer/Life Magazine © Time Inc., (right) The MZTV Museum of Television, Toronto, Ont.; (right inset) Corbis/Bettmann
18: (right) © Disney Enterprises, Inc.
19: © Cecil Stoughton
20: © Stanley Tretick/Corbis Sygma
21: (above left) Corbis/Reuters Newmedia Inc.
23: (below) © Robin Donina Serne, courtesy Florida International Museum (www.floridamuseum.org)

26: (diagram) Dan Fell
28: © Corbis
29: (above) © Keystone/Corbis Sygma
30: (above left) © Bettmann/Corbis
33: (above left) Clive Champion; (below) Corbis/Bettmann
34: (left) Archive Photos; (above) © Keystone/Corbis Sygma
35: (left) Art Rickerby/Life Magazine © Time Inc.; (above) RCMP; (below) © Corbis
36: (diagram) Robert Nicholson/NGS Image Collection; (middle) © The Mark Shaw Collection/Photo Researchers, Inc.; (below) White House Historical Association
38: © Corbis
39: (above) © Corbis Sygma
40: © B. Kraft/Corbis Sygma
41: (above left) © Corbis; (above right) © Corbis; (below) AP/Wide World Photos
43: (above) George Tames/New York Times; (below) © Corbis

44: (left middle, below) © Corbis; (right) Private Collection
47: © Corbis
48: (above right) © Bob Davidoff/Corbis Sygma; (below) © The Mark Shaw Collection/Photo Researchers, Inc.
49: (right middle) © Eugene Allen
50: (above) Tichnor Bros. Inc.
52: © Corbis/Bettmann
55: (above) Art Rickerby/Life Magazine © Time Inc.; (below) © Corbis
56: Bob Gomel/Life Magazine © Time Inc.
57: (left) © Corbis; (right) Mikki Ansin/Liaison Agency
58: (left and right below) © Fred Ward/Black Star; (right above) Mikki Ansin/Liaison Agency
59: © Corbis/Bettmann
62: © Sipa Press
Front cover: John F. Kennedy Library
Back cover: © Corbis and John F. Kennedy Library
Endpapers: © B. Kraft/Corbis Sygma

Selected Bibliography

A Kid's Guide to the White House by Betty Debnam (Andrews McMeel, 1997)

As We Remember Her by Carl Sferrazza Anthony (HarperCollins, 1997)

In the Kennedy Style by Letitia Baldrige (Doubleday, 1998)

Jacqueline Kennedy: The White House Years by Mary van Rensselaer Thayer (Little, Brown, 1971)

John F. Kennedy, President by Hugh Sidey (Atheneum, 1963)

John Fitzgerald Kennedy . . . As We Remember Him edited by Joan Meyers (Atheneum, 1965)

Life in Camelot: The Kennedy Years edited by Philip B. Kunhardt, Jr. (Little, Brown, 1988)

The Memories of Cecil Stoughton and Chester V. Clifton narrated by Hugh Sidey (W.W. Norton, 1980)

My Twelve Years with John F. Kennedy by Evelyn Lincoln (David McKay, 1965)

Prince Charming: The John F. Kennedy, Jr., Story by Wendy Leigh (Dutton, 1993)

Upstairs at the White House by J. B. West (Coward, McCann & Geoghegan, 1973)

The Way We Were by Robert MacNeil (Carroll & Graf, 1988)

The White House: An Historic Guide by the White House Historical Association (National Geographic Society, 1995). The original guide, published in 1962, was Mrs. Kennedy's idea.

White House Nannie by Maud Shaw (New American Library, 1966). Miss Shaw wrote this book after she retired and returned to England to live.

With Kennedy by Pierre Salinger (Jonathan Cape, 1966)

Websites
John F. Kennedy Library
   www.cs.umb.edu/jfklibrary
White House www.whitehouse.gov
White House Historical Association
   www.whitehousehistory.org

Acknowledgments

Madison Press Books and Laurie Coulter are grateful for the assistance of Letitia Baldrige, Rex Scouten, Allan Goodrich of the John F. Kennedy Library, Cecil Stoughton, and Nan Froman. Oral histories from the John F. Kennedy Library consulted include: Letitia Baldrige, Maud Shaw, Nancy Tuckerman, and Pamela Turnure.